# It Looked
# Like Spilt Milk

## by Charles G. Shaw

HarperCollins*Publishers*

IT LOOKED LIKE SPILT MILK

*Copyright, 1947, by Charles G. Shaw*

ISBN 0-06-025566-8
ISBN 0-06-025565-X (lib. bdg.)
ISBN 0-06-443159-2 (pbk.)
L.C. Card 47-30767

11  12  13  SCP  30  29

Sometimes it looked
like Spilt Milk.
But it wasn't Spilt Milk.

Sometimes it looked
like a Rabbit.
But it wasn't a Rabbit.

Sometimes it looked

like a Bird.

But it wasn't a Bird.

Sometimes it looked

like a Tree.

But it wasn't a Tree.

Sometimes it looked
like an Ice Cream Cone.
But it wasn't an Ice Cream Cone.

Sometimes it looked
like a Flower.
But it wasn't a Flower.

Sometimes it looked

like a Pig.

But it wasn't a Pig.

Sometimes it looked
    like a Birthday Cake.
But it wasn't a Birthday Cake.

Sometimes it looked
like a Sheep.
But it wasn't a Sheep.

Sometimes it looked

　　　like a Great Horned Owl.

But it wasn't a Great Horned Owl.

Sometimes it looked
like a Mitten.
But it wasn't a Mitten.

Sometimes it looked
like a Squirrel.
But it wasn't a Squirrel.

Sometimes it looked
like an Angel.
But it wasn't an Angel.

Sometimes it looked
   like Spilt Milk.
But it wasn't Spilt Milk.

It was just a Cloud in the Sky.